Little
RAINDROP

AUTUMN
PUBLISHING

Published in 2022
First published in the UK by Autumn Publishing
An imprint of Igloo Books Ltd
Cottage Farm, NN6 0BJ, UK
Owned by Bonnier Books
Sveavägen 56, Stockholm, Sweden
www.autumnpublishing.co.uk

0522 007
2 4 6 8 10 9 7 5 3
ISBN 978-1-83852-650-4

Illustrated by Gina Maldonado
Written by Melanie Joyce

Designed by Lee Italiano
Edited by Emily Bruce

Printed and manufactured in China

Little
RAINDROP

AUTUMN
PUBLISHING

When I was a raindrop,
I lived up in a cloud.

One day, Thunder rumbled by and **BOOMED** out very **loud.**

"Come now, little raindrops, get ready to let go. You've got important work to do down in the world below."

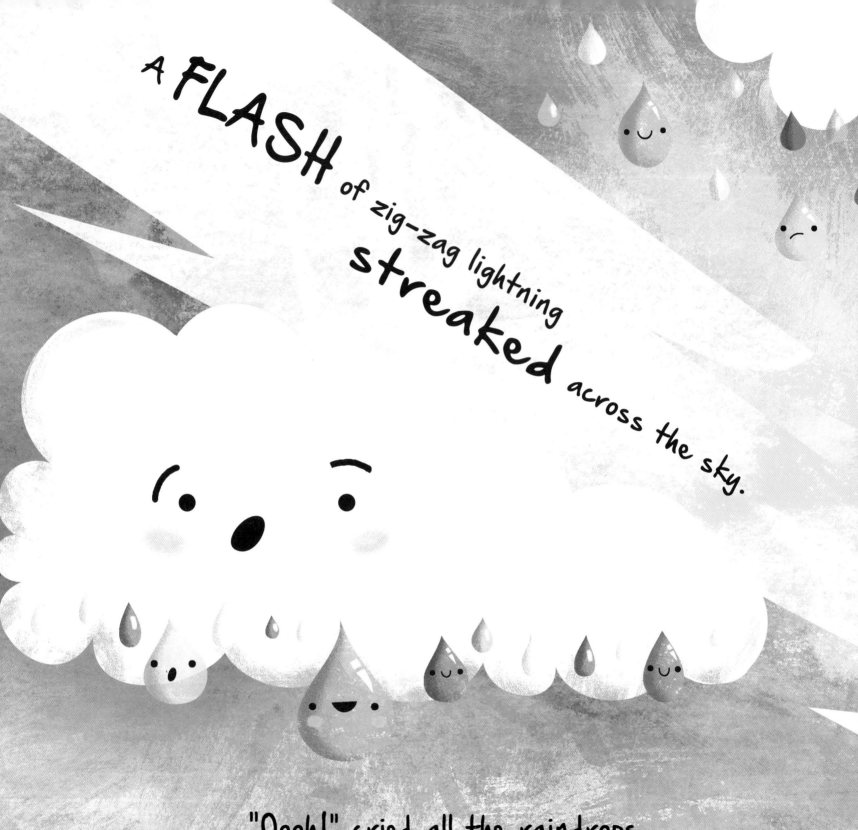

A FLASH of zig-zag lightning streaked across the sky.

"Oooh!" cried all the raindrops.
"See you later, Cloud. Goodbye!"

They jumped into the air, and I jumped with them too.

"Have fun,"
said Cloud.
"I wish that I could
come along with you!"

Down and down we fell, giggling, shouting, "Wheee!"

Oh, what fun to be a raindrop flying free.

From high up in the sky, we saw the earth below.

Sunbeams shone through us and made a lovely big rainbow.

After that,
quite suddenly,
I landed with a

SPLAT!

And dribbled down the tail

I saw a friendly mole,
who was digging by some shoots.

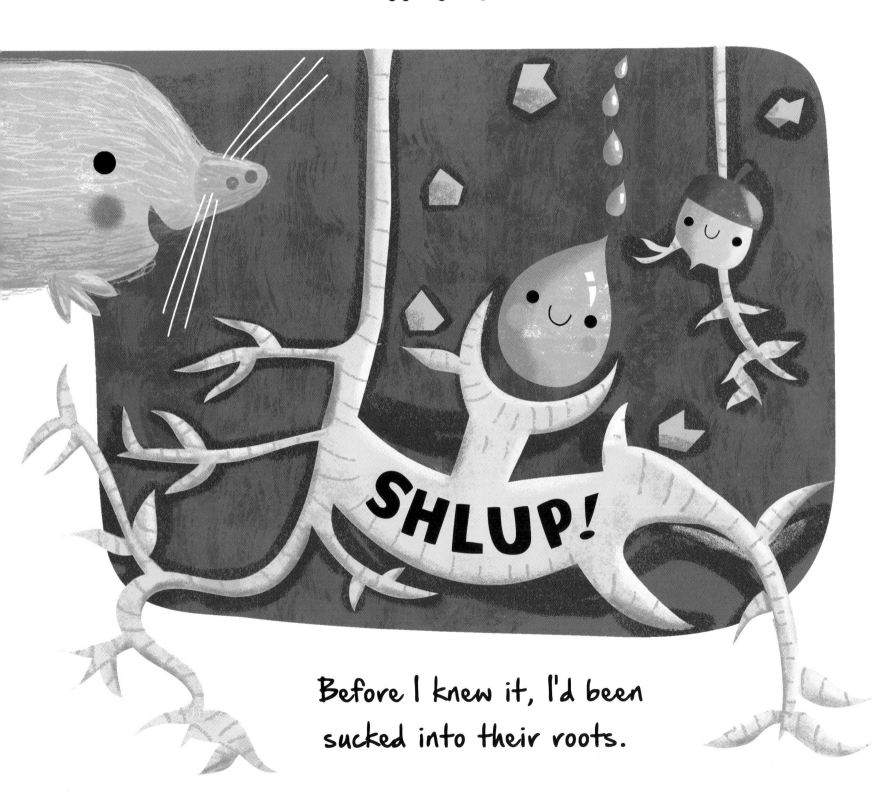

Before I knew it, I'd been
sucked into their roots.

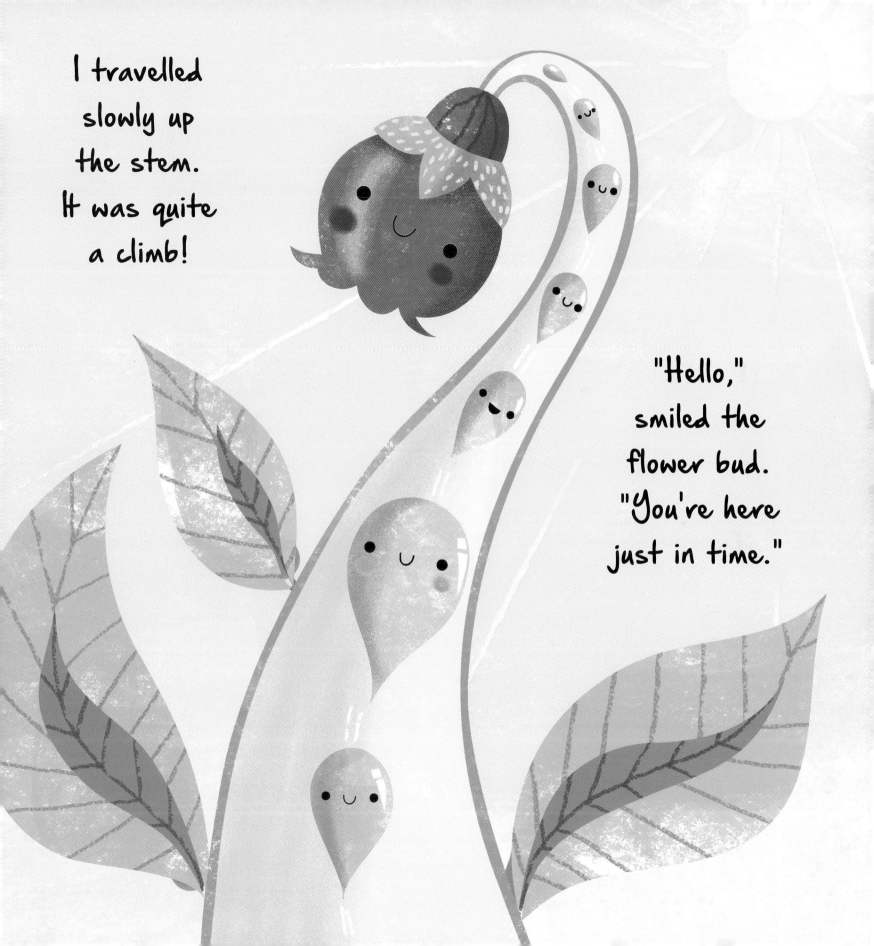

I travelled slowly up the stem. It was quite a climb!

"Hello," smiled the flower bud. "You're here just in time."

"This way," the flower told me, and then it opened wide.
What a nice surprise to see my raindrop friends inside!

We had so much fun, sharing stories of our day,
as the warm sun slowly set, and the light faded away.

We tried to count the stars, instead of counting sheep,
but the petals were so comfy that
we all fell fast asleep.

When the morning came, the sun shone

hot and bright.

We all felt quite peculiar, sort of wibbly and light.

Slowly we drifted upwards,
there was no way to resist.

For I and all my raindrop friends
had turned into a mist.

"What's happening?" I asked,
floating higher with the crowd.

The others laughed and said,
"We're going back into our cloud!"

"Welcome back," said Cloud.

"I hope you all had fun. It's time for you to rest, now that there's lots of sun."

"But soon the wind will blow again,
and turn the weather vane.

And you'll have more adventures,
next time it starts to...

"...rain!"

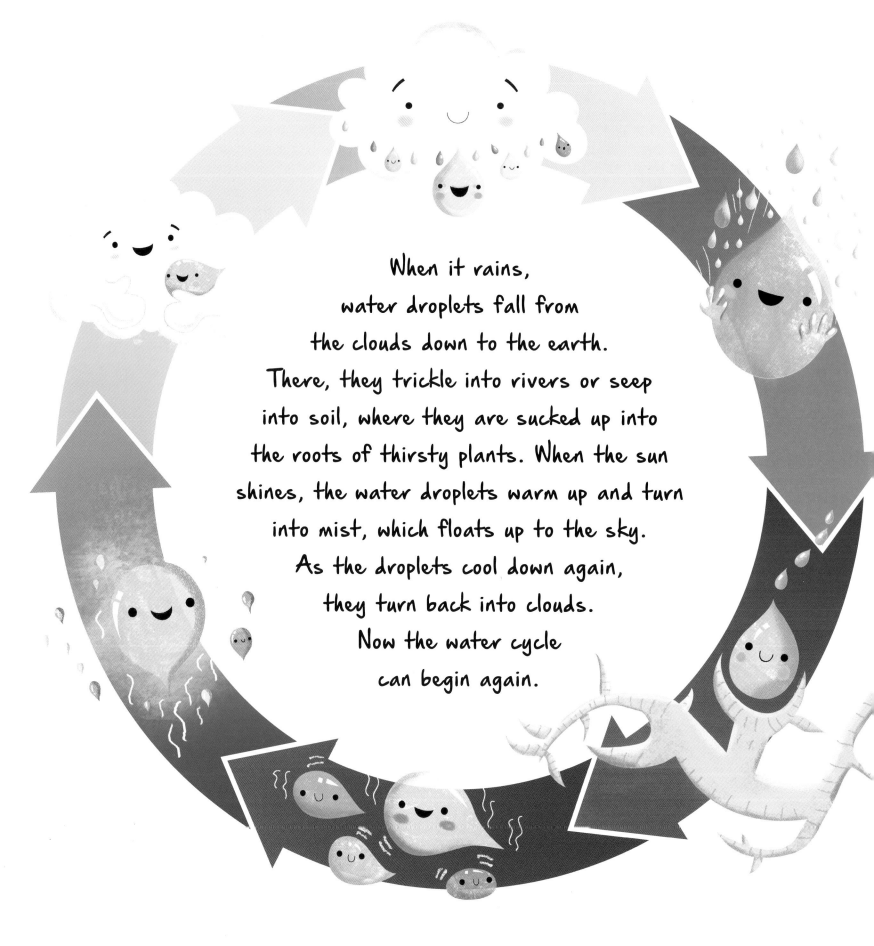

When it rains,
water droplets fall from
the clouds down to the earth.
There, they trickle into rivers or seep
into soil, where they are sucked up into
the roots of thirsty plants. When the sun
shines, the water droplets warm up and turn
into mist, which floats up to the sky.
As the droplets cool down again,
they turn back into clouds.
Now the water cycle
can begin again.